𝔐onday 𝔓opular 𝔠oncerts.

DIRECTOR—Mr. S. ARTHUR CHAPPELL.

THE 500ᵀᴴ CONCERT.*

PROGRAMME FROM WORKS BY

𝔐endelssohn,

the whole of which were performed at the First Monday Popular
Concert, on February 14, 1859.

MONDAY EVENING, JANUARY 18th, 1875.

---

* Fifteenth Concert of the Seventeenth Season.

Part I

QUINTET, in B flat, Op. 87, for two Violins, two Violas, and Violoncello. *Mendelssohn.*

(Eighteenth performance at the Popular Concerts.)

Allegro vivace—B flat major.
Andante scherzando—G minor.
Adagio e lento—D minor.
Allegro molto vivace—B flat major.

Madame NORMAN-NÉRUDA, Herr L. RIES,
Herr STRAUS, Mr. ZERBINI, and Signor PIATTI.

Nothing can be more interesting than a comparison between this quintet—which ranks among the grandest inspirations and most perfect artistic achievements of the gifted master's riper age—and its predecessor, the Quintet in A major, Op. 18, composed in 1826 (nearly 20 years earlier), when Mendelssohn was in his 17th year. And yet they possess little in common beyond their rare perfection as works of art. In comparing the earlier with some of the later works of Mendelssohn, we are not more struck with the genius that could conceive and accomplish the first, in mere boyhood, than at the unabated vigour and wealth of imagination which, nearly a quarter of a century later, engendered such spontaneous, beautiful, and eminently *young* ideas as those abounding in the last. Precocious talent is for the most part either short-lived, or fades with the advance of years; but the invention of Mendelssohn never waxed dim; while as a master he continually progressed, until—when actively employed on several works of importance, among others on the opera of *Loreley,* and especially on what he intended should be his *chef-d'œuvre* (the oratorio of *Christus*)—he was taken away.

The leading themes of each movement of the Quintet in B flat may be indicated by brief citations.

Allegro vivace (leading theme).

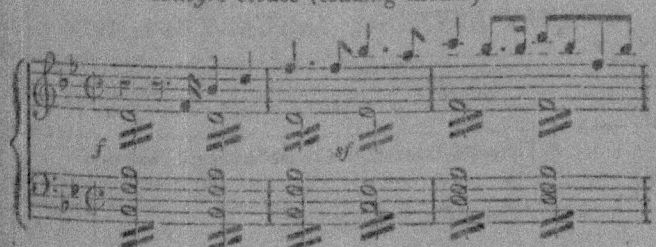

When the full close in B flat is attained, the theme is continued as follows:—

The interrupted cadence (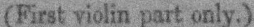) thus brings in an episode, in triplets, which, attentive hearers will not fail to remark, plays a very important part in the development and colouring of the entire movement. Its further progress leads in due course to a resumption of the principal theme, as follows :—

(First violin part only.)

The second theme is given out in the orthodox dominant (F), by the principal viola :—

(Second theme—melody and bass only.)

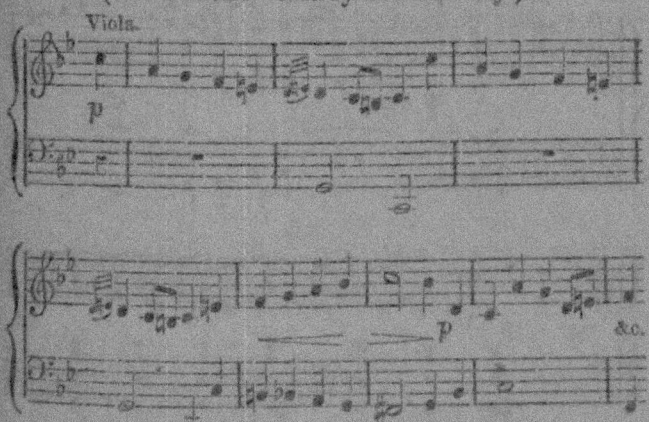

—the first violin immediately taking up the melody, in another key :—

We have then again the ever-busy triplets :—

(First violin part only.)

—the development of the subject giving increased spirit to the movement.

Further on, there is a bold allusion to the leading theme, in a newly harmonised form :—

This, after a full close in F, is again associated with the irrepressible triplets :—

—which, with a striking passage for all the five instruments in unison, bring in, unexpectedly, an episode, still built upon the leading theme, accompanied in *arpeggio* accompaniment by the first violin:—

The dominant key (F) is subsequently resumed, and we then have a peroration, built upon the second theme:—

(Peroration—melody and bass only.)

This first part is not repeated; the second part, or "free fantasia," into which the great masters were accustomed to put all their strength, beginning as follows:—

This important section of the *allegro vivace* is exclusively worked out of the materials already cited. That the second part of the movement, though, of course, more elaborate, is in no degree less spontaneous than the first, must strike every attentive observer. The leading theme is re-introduced, *fortissimo*, in the original key, the second violin, instead of the first, now taking the initiative:—

(Surely, in thinking of this theme, Mendelssohn must have been in some way haunted by the duet between Leonora and Florestan, at the close of the second act of *Fidelio*.) The rest follows in the order to which the great "classical" masters have accustomed us, with certain modifications of not sufficient importance to point out. The movement is brought to an end, *fortissimo*, by a *coda* built upon the leading theme :—

(Coda.)

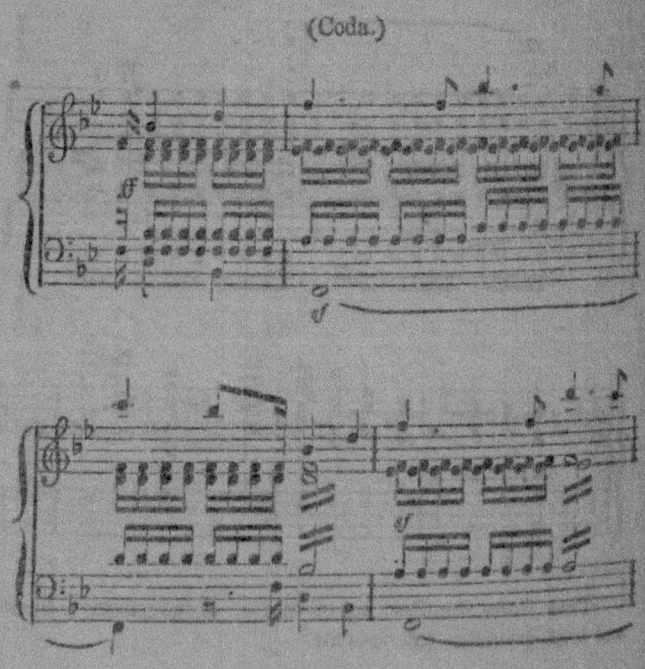

Thus closes the first act of one of Mendelssohn's finest, and most dramatic, tone-poems.

Andante scherzando (leading theme).

(Continuation—melody and bass only.)

(Episode.)

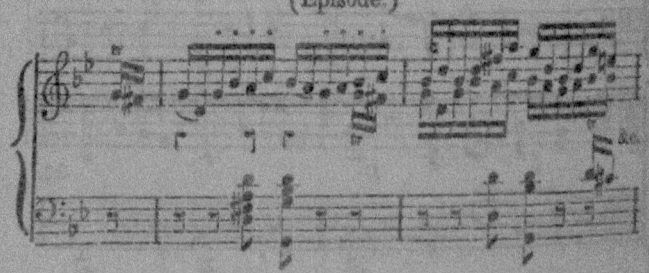

(Second theme—B flat.)

After a brief, but interesting, second part, the leading theme returns in the primary key :—

(Theme—melody and bass only.)

The episode re-appears in due course, now in the key of the dominant :—

(Episode—melody and bass only.)

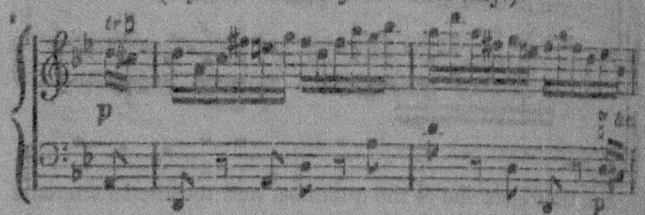

The second theme, coming back in G major, is again allotted to the principal viola :—

(Second theme—melody only.)

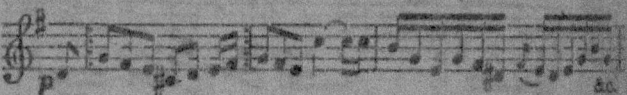

The leading theme returns again in the primary key :—

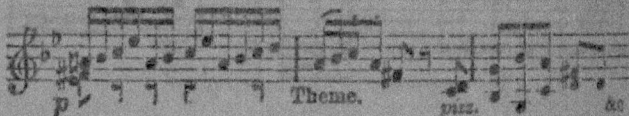

Then, after a new development, the continuation, also in a new form :—

And thus ends one of the quaintest and most characteristic of the whole Mendelssohn family of *scherzi*.

Adagio e lento (leading theme).

(Preamble to leading theme.)

(Second theme—A major.)

The theme being dismissed with unusual brevity, the leading subject returns, in a new key, and with a new accompaniment:—

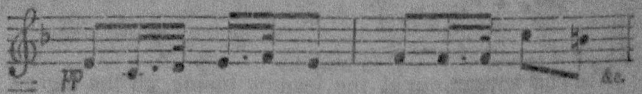

—and this, elaborately developed, is mixed up with episodical matter which must speak for itself. The theme comes back in the original key, with a new florid accompaniment for the first violin :—

The melodious second theme returns in the key of D major, and is now announced by the violoncello :—

Second theme—(melody only.)

The final appearance of the leading theme, on the higher range of the first violin, deserves close attention, as one of the most impressive passages since the last quartets of Beethoven :—

4 L

(Melody only.)

To the *tremolando* accompaniment of the other four instruments it scarcely needs calling attention, or to the change from the minor to the major key, at bar 8 (𝄢). In the major key this fine *adagio* terminates, the *coda*, shortly after the *fortissimo* climax, beginning thus peacefully:—

It may be followed to the end without the aid of further quotation.

This movement, like that of the stringed quartet in F minor ("Posthumous")—shows how nearly Mendelssohn was approaching Beethoven in the last years that were granted to him.

There remains only space for some very brief indications of the materials of which the spirited and admirable *finale* is built.

Finale, molto vivace (leading theme.)

(Continuation.)

(Preamble to second theme.)

(Second theme—F major.)

This theme is then repeated by the first and second violins, to the accompaniment of sustained harmony. Shortly afterwards the leading theme comes back in the primary key. Then follows the "free fantasia," in which the motives cited are elaborately worked out, both separately and in combination. This must be allowed to make its own impression. Never, perhaps, has Mendelssohn exhibited more vigour, unless, perhaps, in the *finale* to his Quartet in E flat, Op. 44, a work conceived and wrought out much in the same spirit.

A peculiar interest attaches to the Quintet in B flat, inasmuch as it is the piece which opened the first Monday Popular Concert, when the Monday Popular Concerts assumed the shape they have adopted since 1859. At the 500th performance it has a just right to the place of honour.

Though a posthumous publication, this Quintet was finished before the oratorio of *Elijah* had been actually begun, and in the catalogue of Rietz stands next to the *Œdipus von Colonos*. It was written for the most part (if not entirely) at Soden, near Frankfort-on-the-Maine, a favourite resort of Mendelssohn's in the summer. No reference is made to it in the published letters of the composer.

TWO-PART SONG. *Mendelssohn.*

Mlle. NITA GAÉTANO and Miss ALICE FAIRMAN.

"THE SABBATH MORN." (SONTAGSMORGEN.)

This is the Sabbath morn!
I am alone within the dell,
Yet one faint sound, the matin bell;
Now still is wood and lawn.

Kneeling, I pray to Thee!
Soft breezes breathe a hallow'd sound;
I feel as though all nature round
Were bound in pray'r with me.

Above, what glories play,
Seeming as though the fields of light
Were open'd to my wond'ring sight;
This is the Sabbath day!

Mendelssohn may justly be denominated the Schubert of the "two-part song;" and probably none of the many specimens he has given to the world of this agreeable form of vocal chamber-music is more genuine and beautiful than the above.

SONATA in F minor (Op. 4), for Pianoforte
and Violin.   *Mendelssohn.*

(Second performance at the Popular Concerts.)

Adagio—Recitativo.
Allegro Moderato—F minor.
Poco Adagio—A flat.
Allegro agitato—F minor.

Miss AGNES ZIMMERMANN and
Madame NORMAN-NERUDA.

It may be reasonably concluded from the character of this
sonata (the only work of the kind by Mendelssohn which
has been published), that the actual date of its production
must be earlier than that of even his three quartets, marked
" Op. 1" in the catalogue. Though a composition of decided
merit, it presents scarcely a trace of that striking individuality
by which nearly everything else we know of Mendelssohn's
is unmistakably distinguished. " I will not"—says an able
and eloquent critic,* in his analysis of the quartet in A
minor, Op. 13—" repeat the argument which this discrepancy
between the order of publication and the order of composition, in Mendelssohn's works, naturally suggests against the
suppression of a quantity of the music he left in manuscript;
but I will urge that the insight the present production affords
us into the state of wonderfully precocious development to
which, while he was still a boy, our composer's mental
powers had attained, gives us the strongest reason to believe,
that any work of his which is withheld from us, is a loss
above value to the art and to the world."

Since the foregoing was written (February, 1859), the
second volume of Mendelssohn's letters has been published,
and in the chronological catalogue appended to it drawn up
by Dr. Julius Rietz, one of the composer's intimate friends,
we find that the Sonata in F minor was first published at
Berlin in 1823, between the second and third of the quartets
to which reference has been made. Mendelssohn must there-
fore have been in his fifteenth year when it was composed.

* Mr. G. A. Macfarren.

A characteristic of this sonata coming from one so young, is its absolute symmetry of form—a symmetry so remarkable, that had the work been signed by Haydn or Mozart no one would have questioned its authenticity. Very few citations may suffice to aid the attention of an intelligent listener.

Introductory Recitative.

Allegro moderato (leading theme).

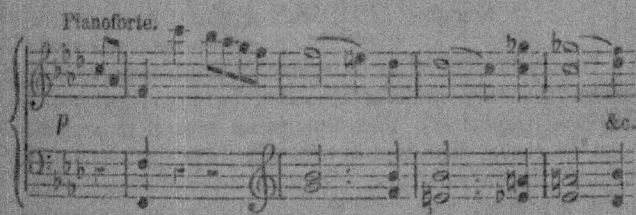

The violin then takes up the theme.

(Episode—Preamble to second theme.)

(Second theme—introduced on the dominant pedal of A flat.)

The violin repeats the melody.

(Peroration to first part—on tonic pedal.)

Out of these materials the *allegro moderato* is exclusively constructed. The second theme (again on a dominant pedal) follows, in the major of the primary:—

(Melody only.)

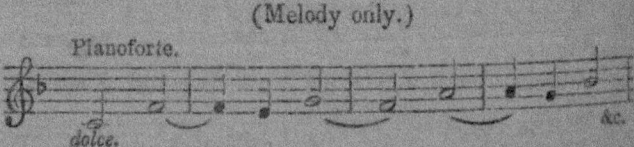

Then, the violin takes it up, as before, and the peroration now re-appears in the primary key—F minor:—

We have afterwards (as in the *coda* to the first part) a reference to the leading theme:—

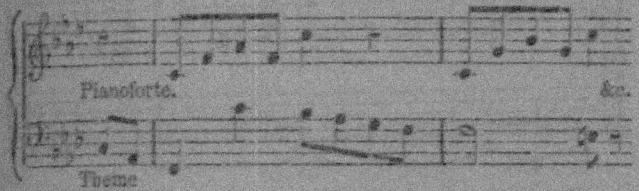

And the movement comes thus tranquilly to an end:—

Adagio (leading theme.)

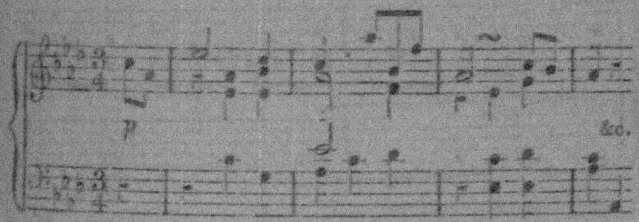

(Second theme—E flat—melody only.)

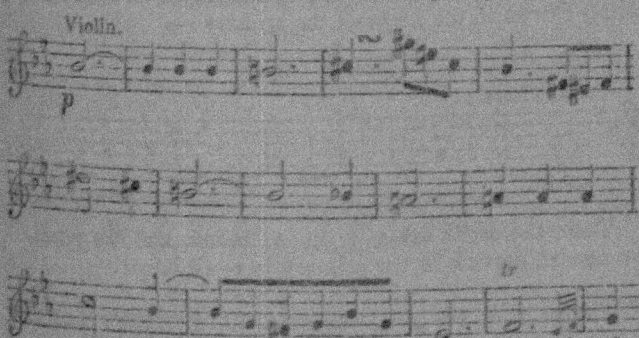

4 M

(New episode.)

This episode is developed at considerable length. The leading theme comes back in the primary key, with florid accompaniment for the violin, which will speak for itself:—

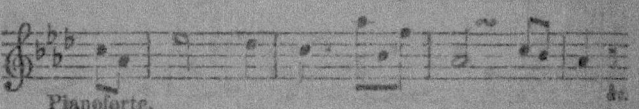

Pianoforte.

The second theme re-appears in a new key:—

(Melody only.)

—and, like the leading *allegro moderato*, the *adagio* ends tranquilly—*diminuendo*.

Allegro agitato (leading theme).

Pianoforte.

The violin answers in due course.

(Second theme—A flat major.)

The working out of the foregoing (the leading theme especially) forms the subject-matter of the entire move-movement.

Near the end, another passage of recitative, for the violin :—

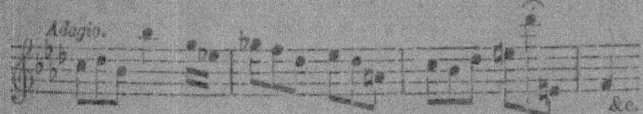

—leads to the *coda*, built upon the leading theme. This, it will be remarked, is fiery and energetic throughout, till the very last bars, which bring the *finale* to an end, just in the same subdued and tranquil manner as its precursors. The concluding four bars are all that can be quoted :—

In his catalogue of Mendelssohn's unpublished works, Herr Julius Rietz—besides a pianoforte concerto, a violin concerto, a pianoforte quartet, a pianoforte trio, and other pieces—names a sonata for pianoforte and tenor (viola), another for pianoforte and clarionet (which ought straightway to be placed in the safe keeping of Mr. Lazarus), and two sonatas for pianoforte and violin, one in D minor, the other in F—with the last of which, bearing the date "1838" (two years after the production of *St. Paul*), all the musical world would only be too charmed to make acquaintance.

END OF THE FIRST PART.

₊ Miss AGNES ZIMMERMANN will perform on one of Messrs. JOHN BROADWOOD and SONS' Concert Grand Pianofortes.

l

SATURDAY POPULAR CONCERTS, ST. JAMES'S HALL.—On Saturday afternoon, January 23, the Programme will include Haydn's Quartet in C major, Op. 20, No. 2, for Strings; Hummel's Sonata for Pianoforte and Violoncello, in A major; Beethoven's Sonata in E flat, Op. 12, No. 3, for Pianoforte and Violin; and Beethoven's Sonata in D minor, for Pianoforte alone. Executants, Mdlle. MARIE KREBS, Madame NORMAN-NÉRUDA, MM. STRAUS, L. RIES, and PIATTI. Vocalist, Mr. GREAVES. Conductor, Sir JULIUS BENEDICT. To commence at Three o'Clock.

Subscription Tickets, to the Sofa Stalls, for the 7 Morning Concerts, taking place on Saturdays, January 16, 23, 30, February 6, 13, 20, and 27, at £1 10s.

Sofa Stalls, 5s. Balcony, 3s. Admission, 1s. Tickets and Programmes at CHAPPELL & Co.'s, 50, New Bond Street.

Entr' Acte.

500th MONDAY POPULAR CONCERT.

ON the 14th of February, 1859, the following announcement prepared the musical public of London for that species of entertainment which during sixteen years has borne the name and title of the " Monday Popular Concerts ":—

" In commencing a new series of entertainments, the design of which may be understood by reference to the programme of this evening, the Directors of the Monday Popular Concerts wish to endow their undertaking with a more universal character than it has hitherto assumed. The advantages offered by St. James's Hall, and the resources placed at their disposal by the generous patronage they have experienced, will, it is confidently hoped, enable them to carry out their plans with success. So rapidly is the taste for pure and healthy music spreading through all classes of the community, that no enterprise of this kind can hope to prosper for any length of time, much less to obtain permanency, without taking this great social fact into consideration.

" The policy which led to the institution of the Monday Popular Concerts, and which has regulated their management from the beginning, will in no way be subverted by the introduction of a wholly new feature. On the contrary, variety will be gained without sacrificing expediency, and a fresh source of recreation to the public be combined, in all likelihood, with such results as may encourage the Directors to use redoubled efforts for the gratification of their supporters, and still further to enlarge the sphere of musical enjoyment.

" It will be perceived that the programme of this evening's concert is made out from compositions, vocal and instrumental, by one master. This plan, which, after reflection, the Directors have thought proper to adopt, while laying no pretence to absolute novelty,* recommends itself as fittest for the purpose, and best calculated to command attention. In its exclusive application to *Chamber Music*, moreover, the experiment may claim to be regarded as in some measure new; and so rich is the catalogue of vocal and instrumental works bequeathed to us by the great composers in this special branch of their art, so marked by sterling excellence, and thus undeserving of neglect, that, backed by the suffrages of the

---

* M. Jullien is the acknowledged originator of such performances in this country, and has thereby rendered services which ought neither to be forgotten nor undervalued.

public, the Directors of the Monday Popular Concerts have no doubt whatever of being able to present a succession of entertainments unprecedented, at least, in *variety* of attraction. The classical repertory of the stringed quartet, and of the sonata for piano, solos, or accompanied, is immense; while that of the chamber songs, duets and trios, is fairly inexhaustible.

"It is proposed to inaugurate this new experiment by a series of six concerts, each devoted to one, or at most two, of the recognised masters of the art; and, should these performances be honoured by public approval, to renew them at intervals. The Directors have selected Mendelssohn for the first, not with any idea of distinguishing that renowned composer from his illustrious predecessors, but simply because, owing to circumstances upon which it is unnecessary to dwell, the great popularity attached to his name in this country is united to a sympathy almost bordering on affection. The programme selected from his works is a specimen of the plan which will be strictly adhered to, so far as that is possible, in all the future concerts of the series. It includes, as will be observed, two pieces for stringed instruments (a quintet and a quartet); two pieces in which the pianoforte plays a conspicuous part* (a sonata with violin, and an *air varié* with violoncello); two two-part songs for female voices; two four-part songs for male and female voices (soprano, alto, tenor, and bass); two organ solos; and four solo songs, one for each of the principal performers. Thus, it is believed, a certain symmetry of form has been attained, combined with a revelation of the composer's genius and skill in each department of Chamber Music. The whole performance (provided there are no encores) will, it is calculated, allowing for the interval between the parts, occupy somewhere about two hours and a half; and Mendelssohn's capability to entertain and delight a music-loving audience during that space of time, uninterruptedly, has been repeatedly shown, even at the concerts of M. Jullien, where the music has been of a character uniformly serious, and for the most part unrelieved by those lighter vocal pieces which the Directors of the Monday Popular Concerts trust may prove all the more acceptable from their association with such works as the quintet, quartet, and sonata—for which last, earnest and unremitting attention is respectfully solicited.

"In order to render the series of Classical Concerts as attractive as possible, and to give due effect to the music comprised in the programmes, the most eminent available vocal and instrumental talent, foreign and native, will be engaged, and nothing will be left undone by the Directors to make their new undertaking worthy of public support."

The success of the new undertaking may be deduced from the fact that, since the first "Mendelssohn Night," its plan has never been departed from, and that 500 concerts have been given within so comparatively brief a period. The original intention, it need scarcely be said, was to make the

---

* It is scarcely necessary to premise, that compositions for pianoforte alone will be prominent features in the series.

general public acquainted with those masterpieces of the musical art of which only a very few had been previously known, except to select circles—and even to select circles, probably, not one out of fifty. A glance at the annually printed "Catalogue of Works performed at the Monday Popular Concerts" will suffice to show that, to the best of the Director's ability, the scheme has been carried out in accordance with the spirit that originated it. The catalogue refers to between 500 and 600 compositions, the majority of which are by the recognised great masters, from Bach and Handel to Haydn and Mozart, from Haydn and Mozart to Cherubini and Beethoven, and from these last to Spohr, Weber, Schubert, Mendelssohn, Schumann, and Sterndale Bennett. The eminent artists who have taken part in the performances, and materially led to their success, need not be signalised by name. It is the Director's hope that, by adhering to the policy hitherto guiding him, he may continue to deserve the kind and liberal support which encouraged him at the outset of his undertaking, and has never yet been withheld.

S. A. C.

500th MONDAY POPULAR CONCERT.

(From the "Musical World," January 11th.)

On Monday next will take place in St. James's Hall the 500th Concert of the series begun, under Mr. S. Arthur Chappell's management, on February 14, 1859. By a happy decision, the programme then put forward will in great part be presented again, but not in conjunction with the same performers. Of the artists who appeared in 1859 only three—Sir J. Benedict, Herr Ries, and Signor Piatti—are announced for Monday next. M. Wieniawski is in Brussels, Mr. Doyle has long terminated his connection with Mr. Chappell's enterprise, and M. Schreurs has disappeared from public life. The three who remain at their posts, however, suffice for a personal link between the first concert and its 500th successor, the marvel being that, amid the constant changes which take place in the musical world, so many of the original performers are available. Under circumstances of such interest, it may not be out of place to reproduce the notice of the first concert from the number of the *Musical World* for February 19, 1859, simply premising that Mr. Chappell had been giving a series of miscellaneous performances, which the "Monday Pops," as we now know them, succeeded:—

"It might have been imagined that some hazard would attend the new policy of the directors of these entertainments in giving a series of classical concerts so soon after the 'miscellaneous.' The directors, however, proved the best judges, and the success of last Monday night's performance may justify them in believing that they hit upon the most orthodox way of pleasing the public. No doubt there has been a good deal of taste displayed in the experiment. Mendelssohn's name is a tower of strength, and the programme of the first concert was selected entirely from his chamber music. Mendelssohn, unaided, as had been often proved by M. Jullien, was sure to attract the multitude. But there was this drawback, apparently, against the Monday Popular Concerts, that, no band being employed, there could be no symphony and no overture. That chamber music, however, can charm even 'popular' assemblies, was triumphantly proved on the present occasion. The programme was a model of its kind. While conciliating the most refined taste, it was equally calculated to gratify the uninitiated. The grand pieces in each part were the quintet in B flat (Op. 87), and the quartet in D major (Op. 44), for stringed instruments. The first was executed by M. Wieniawski, Herr Ries, Mr. Doyle, M. Schreurs, and Signor Piatti; the second by the same, excluding Mr. Doyle. Both were magnificent performances, and created genuine enthusiasm. The last movement of the quartet was obstinately redemanded, but the compliment was merely acknowledged by the performers. M. Wieniawski's playing was incomparable in the quintet—taste, feeling, expression, style, tone, and execution, all combining to make a perfect whole. His performance in the quartet was extremely fine, although occasional exceptions might be taken to his reading. We need not say how ably M. Wieniawski was supported by his coadjutors. Besides what we have specified, Messrs. Benedict and Wieniawski played the sonata in F minor (Op. 4), for piano and violin, and Mr. Benedict and Signor Piatti the *Tema con variazioni* in D (Op. 17), for piano and violoncello."

How far the tone of encouragement and confidence which appears in this earliest notice of the Monday Popular Concerts has been justified by results we need not stop to point out.

Apropos of the 500th Concert, we are not going to praise the enterprise with which it is associated. The Concert itself is praise enough, inasmuch as everything significant of good management, steady perseverance, and all the merits that command success, may be seen in the figures which designate it. But, while laudation is unnecessary, we cannot refrain from making some reflections suggested by the event of Monday next. In the first place, we see the advantage of quietly working out a good idea, without reference to immediate results. It is no secret that, for several years, the Monday Popular Concerts did not pay their expenses, and had their Director looked only to this fact they would long since have come to an end. But Mr. Chappell had an eye to the future and faith in what it would bring forth. To him the years of loss were only as the time when seed lies hidden beneath the surface of the ground. The harvest was to come, and it came in greater abundance, perhaps, than the most sanguine expected. So will time always fight for a good cause, and for those who, identified with good causes, know how to possess their souls in patience. The 500th Concert testifies, also, the value of firmness and decision in carrying out an artistic enterprise. How far Mr. Chappell has been tempted again and again to depart from his original and severely classical design, only he can tell; but it is easy to assume that no small share of resolution was necessary, in order to keep in the path first marked out. The danger passed away long ago, but

4 N

none the less should the firmness which met it be recognized; and all the more should the fact be insisted on that good things never fail to surround themselves, in course of time, with the sympathy necessary for support. The Monday Popular Concerts have made their own public, to whom they are, so to speak, a necessity. They belong to that public, and Mr. Chappell simply acts as agent, free from risk, while getting what he can for his trouble. This is the reward of years of steady work, looking neither to the right hand nor to the left. Who will say that the reward is too great; or that it is other than a notable encouragement?

The whole subject has such obvious teachings connected with it, and assumes such unmistakeable significance, that nothing more need be said about it. In common with all who desire the good of music, we congratulate the amateurs who are scarcely less interested in it, and we congratulate the art which is most interested of all.   JOSEPH BENNETT.

500th MONDAY POPULAR CONCERT.

(From the *Pall Mall Gazette*.)

The next of the Monday Popular Concerts will possess not only a musical but also something of an historical interest. It will be the 500th Concert since this kind of entertainment—Chamber Music for the public in general—was first invented. The fact may also be regarded with advantage from a statistical point of view. It would take one of our ordinary Musical Societies, giving six Concerts in the course of the year, upwards of eighty years to reach its 500th Concert; and long before the expiration of eighty years the Society would fall to pieces, undergo reconstruction, and fall to pieces again times innumerable. It may be hoped, in the interest of all who enjoy good music, that there will soon be an end to societies whose annual scheme includes six, or at most eight, Concerts. Indeed, nothing is more certain than that Concerts must be given much more frequently than of old if the public are to be expected to take any great interest in them. Regular musical nourishment is what is wanted, not an occasional musical snack six times a year. As for the Monday Popular Concerts, they have gone on increasing in success in proportion as the audiences have become more and more familiarised with the works presented. When they were first begun the great mass of the public were quite ignorant of Chamber Music. Trios and quartets were almost unknown, and there were plenty of amateur pianists whose acquaintance with Beethoven's sonatas was limited to the first movement of the "Moonlight Sonata" and the funeral march of the sonata in A flat. Such amateurs have had the opportunity not merely of hearing, but of hearing again and again some thirty of the sonatas, together with nearly all the duets, trios, quartets, quintets, &c. (the septet was already tolerably well known) of the greatest of instrumental composers. Some of the more determined frequenters may be said to have received at the Monday Popular Concerts a regular musical education; for almost as much may be learned of music by carefully listening to it as of books by carefully reading them.

The 500th Concert is, appropriately enough, to be a reproduction of the first Monday Popular Concert ever given, when the programme was made up entirely of works by Mendelssohn. This reminds us that for the first few years it seemed to be a fundamental "Monday Popular" idea that each Concert should be devoted to the works of one and the same composer. The idea was a good one, and possibly the director may now from time to time revert to it. It will be interesting, in any ——— to hear next Monday a Concert of the original pattern. The varied character of the programmes of the present time must be more attractive to the general public, but there was a good deal to be said for the old style of programme, which, if the Monday Popular Concerts were addressed to students alone, would certainly be the best of the two. We are under the impression that Schubert did not become a great name at the Monday Popular Concerts until the one-composer system had been abandoned. In that case, one Schubert Concert ought to be given, when it would doubtless be seen that, though admiration may be more readily expressed for other masters—greater, perhaps, than he—there is no master amongst those termed " classical " so much liked as this wonderful song-writer, who, for whatever instrument or combination of instruments he happened to be composing, still wrote songs.

Part II

TEMA CON VARIAZIONI, for Pianoforte and
Violoncello, Op. 17.   *Mendelssohn.*

(Ninth performance at the Popular Concerts.)

Andante con moto	(tema)		D major.
,, ,, ,,	(1st variation)		,, ,,
,, ,, ,,	(2nd ,,	)	,, ,,
Più vivace	(3rd ,,	)	,, ,,
Allegro con fuoco	(4th ,,	)	,, ,,
L'istesso tempo	(5th ,,	)	,, ,,
,, ,,	(6th ,,	)	,, ,,
Presto ed agitato	(7th ,,	)	D minor.
Tempo primo	(8th ,,		,, major.
,, ,,	(Coda)		,, ,,

Miss AGNES ZIMMERMANN and Signor PIATTI.

This *Tema con Variazioni* was composed at Berlin, in
1828, for the late Herr Paul Mendelssohn, the author's
brother, an amateur violoncello player of considerable skill.
Mendelssohn is believed to have written another piece of the
same kind; but there is no reference to it in the catalogue
of Herr Julius Rietz.

The theme upon which these variations are constructed is
as follows :—

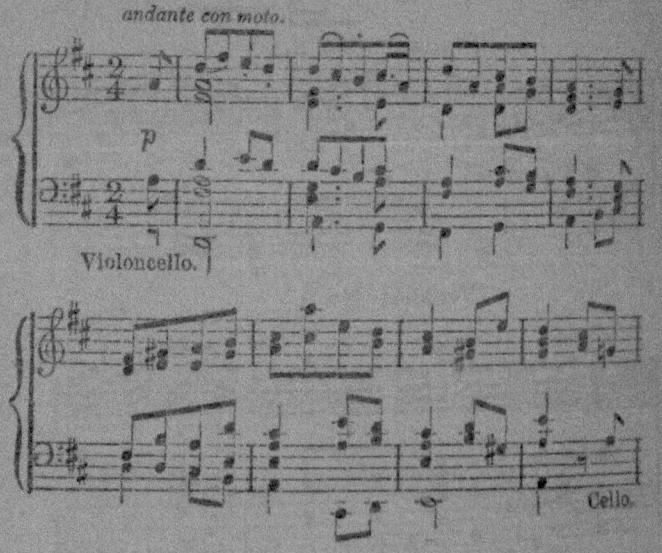

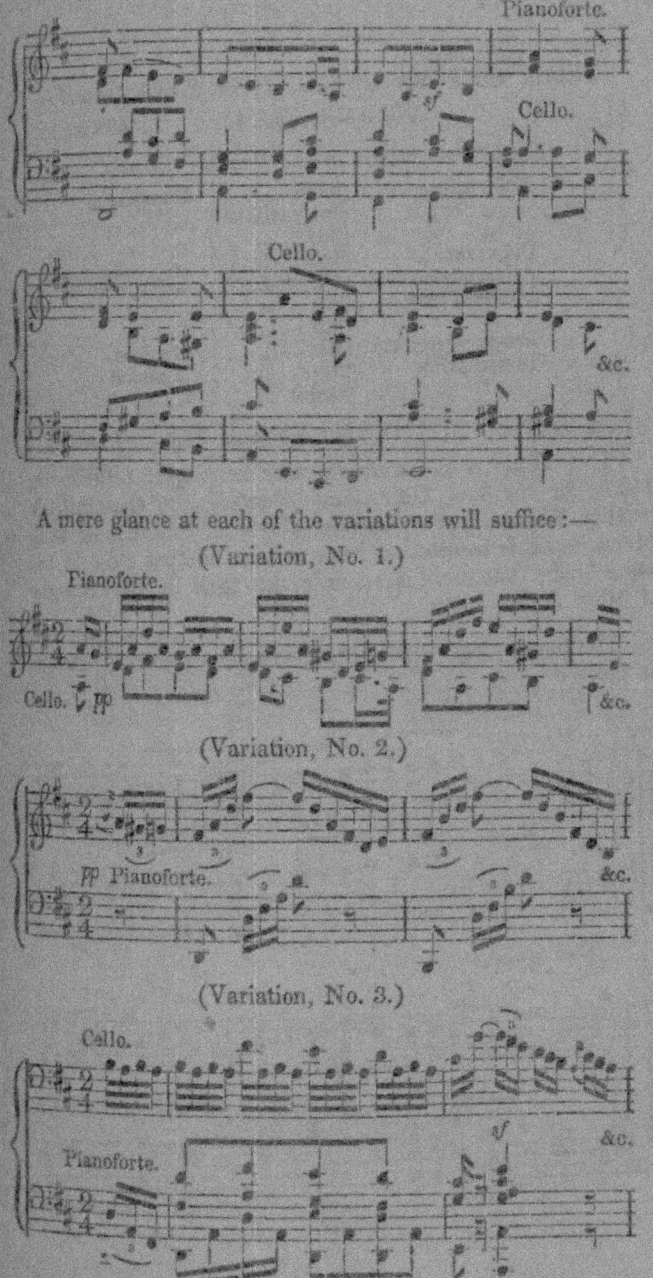

A mere glance at each of the variations will suffice:—

(Variation, No. 1.)

(Variation, No. 2.)

(Variation, No. 3.)

(Variation, No. 4.)

(Variation, No. 5.)

(Variation, No. 6.)

(Variation, No. 7—minor key—melody and bass only.)

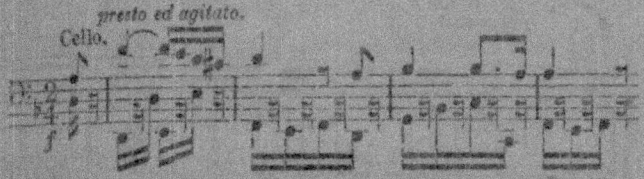

The pianoforte accompaniment to this variation is in syncopated chords.

(Variation, No. 8.)

It will be remarked that in the last variation the violoncello sustains a note (A) throughout the entire duration of the two sections of the melody. The *coda* ("*più animato*"), which follows and brings the whole to an end, will speak for itself.

The *Tema con Variazioni* was first introduced by Mr. (now Sir Julius) Benedict and Signor Piatti, at the first concert of the first season—February 14, 1859.

** The violoncello on which Signor Piatti performs is a genuine Stradivarius of rare quality, formerly in the possession of General Oliver, and presented by that gentleman to the accomplished violoncellist as a token of regard.

TWO-PART SONG. *Mendelssohn.*

Mlle. NITA GAËTANO and Miss ALICE FAIRMAN.

I would that my love could silently
Flow in a single word,
I'd give it the merry breezes,
They'd waft it away in sport.

To thee on their wings, my fairest,
That soul-felt word would bear;
Should'st hear it at ev'ry moment,
And hear it ev'rywhere.

At night, when thine eyelids in slumber
Have clos'd those bright heav'nly beams,
Still there, my love, it will haunt thee,
E'en in thy deepest dreams.

"Ich wollt' Liebe meine ergösse sich all in ein einzig Wort." This is the most widely known, and in England, perhaps, the most popular of the published two-part songs of Mendelssohn.

QUARTET, in D major, Op. 44, No. 1, for two Violins, Viola, and Violoncello. *Mendelssohn.*

(Ninth performance at the Popular Concerts.)

Molto allegro vivace—D major.
Minuetto, un poco allegretto—D major; with
    Trio—B minor.
Andante espressivo, ma con moto—B minor.
Presto con brio—D major.

Madame NORMAN-NÉRUDA,
Herr L. RIES, Herr STRAUS, and Signor PIATTI.

The second volume of Mendelssohn's letters contains a passage (in a letter to Ferdinand David of Leipsic) which shows that when he had completed this quartet—the first (according to the *opus* number) of his Op. 44—he was well pleased with it.* Herr Julius Rietz, one of the four to whom was entrusted the task of examining Mendelssohn's MSS. and preparing them for publication, is quite in the dark about the quartet in D major. The MS. not having been found, Herr

---

* "I have just finished my third quartet in D major, and like it much. May it only please you as well. I almost think it will, for it is more spirited, and seems to me likely to be more grateful to the players than the others." (Lady Wallace's translation of Mendelssohn's Letters from 1833 to 1847.)

Rietz, thinking, perhaps, that it could not by any possibility have travelled out of Germany, does not include it in the regular catalogue, with dates affixed to each composition, but refers to it in his preface, among eleven other works* which he has been unable to arrange chronologically. Mendelssohn, however, came so frequently to England that Herr Rietz might have just thought it likely he had some English friends, to one of the most intimate of whom he had very probably confided the original MS. of the quartet under notice. As it happens, this was really the case. The MS. of the Quartet in D major —like that of the overture, *Die Hebriden (Isles of Fingal)*, according to the version invariably used in public (Herr Moscheles has the other, which is essentially different) — is in the possession of Sir Sterndale Bennett. Herr Rietz positively gives the Quartet in D major, together with five other pieces, to "the last period, *subsequent to* 1840," although No. 2 (in E minor) belongs to 1837, and No. 3 (E flat major) to 1838.†

The opening movement of the Quartet in D major is an *allegro*, of which the subjoined vigorous melody, allotted to the first violin, is the leading subject:—

molto allegro vivace.

---

* The Pianoforte Sonata in E major, the First Symphony (in C minor), and the Second Pianoforte Trio (C minor), are among these. Herr Rietz's doubts about the quartet are the more extraordinary, inasmuch as that he (under Mendelssohn's supervision) arranged all three of the quartets, Op. 44, as duets for the pianoforte, and that these arrangements are published.

† Moreover, the letter addressed to Ferdinand David, in which Mendelssohn says (Lady Wallace's translation, page 154), " I have just finished my third quartet in D major," &c. is dated " Berlin, July 30th, 1828." Surely Herr Rietz must have read the volume of Letters to which he affixed his " Catalogue."

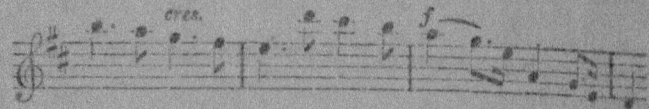

This theme has a tributary, which follows it immediately, in the same key, but of quite an opposite character :—

1st Violin.

After a repetition of the leading theme, the tributary is made the subject of an episode in the dominant key (A):—

And when this is brought to a full close, the second theme appears, in F sharp minor :—

Instead of coming to a close in F sharp minor, the cadence is interrupted thus :—

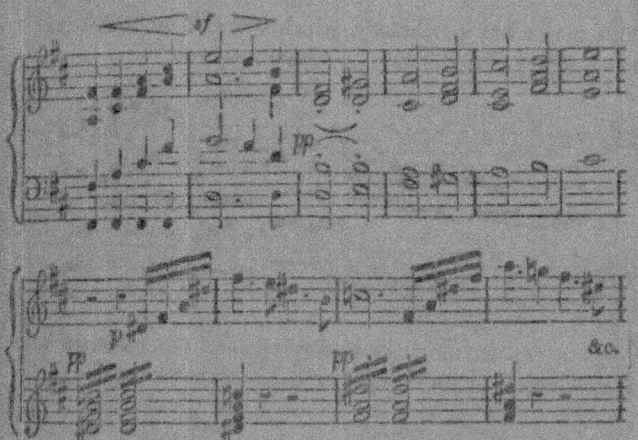

This commences the peroration to the first part, which comprises a fresh theme, as vigorous as that which opens the movement :—

The repetition of the first part is led up to by a spirited passage in the form of a strict canon on the octave :—

In octaves with Viola.

4 P

Out of these materials the *molto allegro vivace* is entirely constructed. The ingenious manner in which they are developed in the course of the second part of the movement will not escape observation.

The theme of the *minuetto* is a charming example of the pastoral style :—

A reference to the *minuetto* of Beethoven's quartet in the same key (Op. 18) will show that Mendelssohn, while writing the foregoing, was in some degree influenced by that graceful inspiration. Not so, however, with the *trio*, which is pure Mendelssohn throughout :—

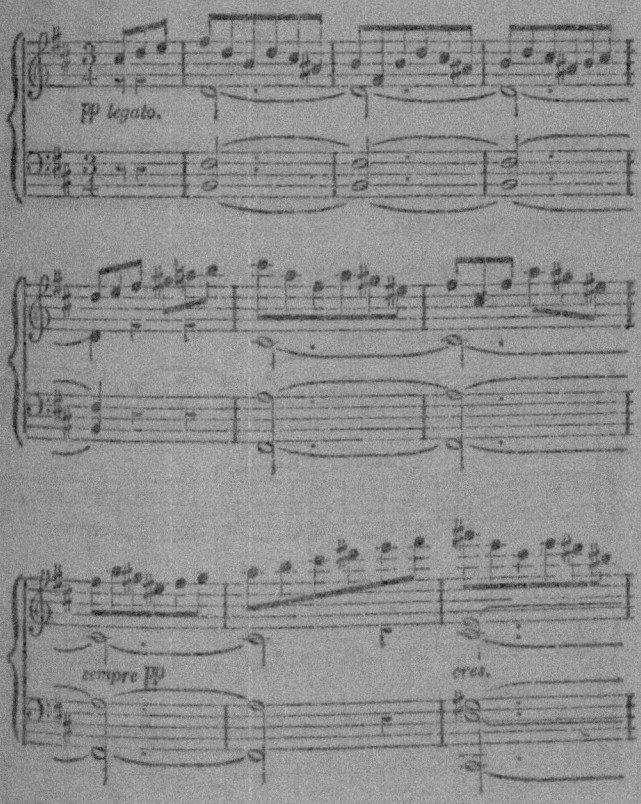

The *andante espressivo con moto* is one of those movements which bear the impress of Mendelssohn's strongly marked individuality from first to last:—

The second subject, in the relative major (D), beginning on a *pedale* of the *six-fourth*, while the semiquaver motion of inner parts is sustained, contrasts happily with the fore-going :—

Towards the end, after a *cadenza solus*, for the first violin, an interesting épisode occurs, from which a brief quotation may suffice :—

Then, with a last look back at the opening theme, this very original movement quietly terminates :—

The final *presto* is quite as animated as the opening *allegro*, and written in a still more elaborate style. The following is its spirited first subject :—

—which is thus continued in a more melodious strain :—

After the working out of this, a striking episode :—

—brings us to the second theme—a tuneful *cantabile* in the dominant key (A) :—

The foregoing are the principal materials upon which the *finale* is built. There is no room for further quotations; nor, indeed, are they necessary. The many striking points will speak for themselves to every attentive hearer.

The three quartets, Op. 44, are amongst the ripest productions of Mendelssohn's second period.

The Quartet in D major was first introduced by Herr Wieniawski, Herr L. Ries, Herr Schreurs, and Signor Piatti, at the first concert of the first season (Feb. 14, 1859), when the entire programme was devoted to Mendelssohn's music.

END OF THE FIVE HUNDREDTH CONCERT.

SATURDAY POPULAR CONCERTS.

SATURDAY AFTERNOON, JAN. 23rd, 1875.

PROGRAMME.

QUARTET, in C major, Op. 20, No. 2, for two Violins, Viola,
and Violoncello .... Haydn.

Madame NORMAN-NÉRUDA,
MM. L. RIES, STRAUS, and PIATTI.

SONG, "Lascia amor" .... Handel.

Mr. GREAVES.

SONATA, in D minor, Op. 29, No. 2, for
Pianoforte alone.. Beethoven.

Madlle. MARIE KREBS.

SONATA, in A major, for Pianoforte and Violoncello .... Hummel.

(First time at the Popular Concerts.)

Madlle. MARIE KREBS and Signor PIATTI.

SONG, "Love leads to battle".................................... Buononcini.

Mr. GREAVES.

SONATA, in E flat, Op. 12, No. 3, for Pianoforte and Violin...Beethoven.

Madlle. MARIE KREBS and Madame NORMAN-NÉRUDA.

Conductor   -   Sir JULIUS BENEDICT.

www.ingramcontent.com/pod-product-compliance
Lightning Source LLC
Chambersburg PA
CBHW081215170626
46811CB00010B/3304